D1597160

Adventure in the City of David

"…The streets of the city
shall be crowded with
boys and girls playing."

ZECHARIAH 8:5

Dedicated to our Beloved
Children, Grandchildren and
Great-Grandchildren

Sue & Barry
Jerusalem, Israel

Adventure
in the
City of David

Ahron Horovitz

Illustrations: Hadas Huri

MEGALIM
CITY OF DAVID-ANCIENT JERUSALEM

MAGGID

Adventure in the City of David
First English Edition, 2015

Megalim, City of David Institute for Jerusalem Studies

© Ir David Foundation, 2015

Graphic design: Stephanie and Ruti Designs
Illustration: Hadas Huri
English translation: Ruchi Avital and Miriam Feinberg Vamosh
English editors: Deborah Stern, Tali Simon
Production manager: Shifi Cohen
Assistant production manager: Lea Neeman

All rights reserved to Ir David Foundation. No part of this publication may be reproduced stored in a retrieval system or transmitted in any form or by any means, electronic, mechanical, photocopying or otherwise, without prior permission from Ir David Foundation, except in the case of a brief quotation embedded in critical articles or reviews.

Maggid Books
A Division of Koren Publishers Jerusalem Ltd.
POB 8531, New Milford, CT 06776, USA
POB 4044, Jerusalem, 91040, Israel
www.korenpub.com

Megalim
City Of David Institute For Jerusalem Studies
www.cityofdavid.org.il
megalim@cityofdavid.org.il

ISBN 978-1-59264-405-6, hardcover original
Printed and Bound in Israel

Biblical Jerusalem in the City of David fascinates millions of people all over the world, but its rich history can be too complicated for the uninitiated, especially young people who often remain oblivious to its treasures. *Adventure in the City of David* is the Megalim Institute's first publication for children. We hope that it will bring them the into the captivating world of ancient Jerusalem and inspire them to continue learning about Jewish history, the Bible, and the City of David.

I would like to express my gratitude to the Silver family of Toronto and the Mizrachi Organization of Canada for their assistance in publishing this book.

Thank you to Shifi Cohen, production manager, and Lea Neeman, who assisted me throughout the writing of this book with their wise advice and artistic talents. Thank you to Ruchi Avital and Miriam Feinberg Vamosh for the translation to English and Debbie Stern for the editing, to Hadas Huri, for her wonderful illustrations, and to Stephanie and Ruti Design, Gali Gamliel Fleischer, Anna Hacco and especially, Tamar Wieder, designer, for their beautiful work.

I would like to thank the Ir David Foundation's co-chairman, Rabbi Yehuda Maly, and the senior director, Doron Spielman, as well as Atara Harow, Matanya Chait, Rita Ganz, Hila Barzilay, Ella Ben-Shitrit, Yael Ginsberg, Eli Aloni, Leora Roth, and especially my staff at the Megalim Institute: Dr. Anat Roth, director, Bracha Reich, and Ofer Avnon.

Finally, many thanks are extended to David (David'le) Beeri, chairman and founder of the Ir David Foundation, whose nickname hints at the youthful exuberance with which he approaches all issues that relate to Jerusalem. David gave his unyielding support to this project. Last but not least, I thank my wife and life partner, Dr. Esther Horovitz, for her warm support and wise advice.

Ahron Horovitz
Senior Director, Megalim Institute

In memory of my mother, Leah Horovitz
The stories she told me as a child
are forever engraved on my heart.

Chapter **1** Uri Gets an Unexpected (and Annoying) **Assignment**

It really wasn't his fault. All Uri wanted to do was tell the teacher *his* theory about how King David had managed to get through the mighty walls of Jerusalem and capture the city from the Jebusites. It was simple. David had made a giant sling, packed his soldiers into it, and then flung them over the walls of Jebus. The soldiers dropped into the city, to the total astonishment of the Jebusites, and took it by surprise.

The class burst out laughing.

"We're discussing a serious matter here, Uri," said the teacher. "For years, scholars have been trying to solve the riddle of how David's small and untrained army took on the mighty Canaanite city of Jebus. Your idea is totally unrealistic. It sounds like a fairy tale. How did you dream this one up?"

"Dreamer, dreamer! Uri the dreamer!" the class pitched in.

"I am not!" Uri shouted back, his face growing hot. "It could have happened like that. You don't understand."

They were making fun of his imagination again, calling him a dreamer. And if he did use his imagination from time to time, so what? Mom said that imagination was the sign of a creative mind.

The commotion in the classroom grew louder and louder. Uri's face turned as red as his hair. Suddenly Yoav jumped up and yelled, "Carrot top! Carrot top!" The whole class joined in the uproar. That's when things really got out of hand.

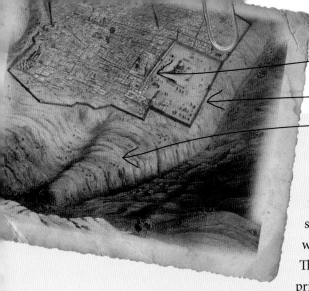

— Western Wall

— Old City walls

— City of David

Later, Uri couldn't remember exactly how he and Yoav hit the floor fighting. He certainly hadn't started it. Well, he hadn't meant to start it, but maybe his temper had gotten the better of him. And who could blame him with the whole class making fun of him? That Yoav! For some reason, it was always Uri who was sent to the principal's office.

"Uri is a great kid, really imaginative," said the principal to Uri's parents, "but his quick temper sometimes gets the better of him. He needs a short leave of absence from school to cool off a bit. Think of it as a three-day field assignment."

A three-day field assignment, thought Uri. Where would I do that?

It was Dad who suggested the City of David. "Maybe you could join Uncle Ronny," he said. "He's in charge of the archaeological excavations in the City of David. You could learn a lot from him about ancient Jerusalem."

"Brilliant," said Uri's teacher excitedly when he told her about his father's suggestion. "The City of David is the ancient core of Jerusalem. It's the seed from which the city grew and developed. Perhaps when you're there, you'll be able to figure out how David really captured Jerusalem from the Jebusites."

Everybody seemed excited about Uri's assignment except Uri. Leaving his friends for three days for some archaeological excavation was not his idea of a good time. But he did like Uncle Ronny and — who knows? — maybe there were hidden treasures to be found underneath the ground. There I go, he scolded himself, letting my imagination run wild again. It'll probably be the most boring three days of my life.

This symbol refers to the map located at the end of the book.
Use it to track Uri as he travels through the City of David.

Chapter 2 Uri Searches for (and Finds) the Lost City

That evening, Uri planned his first visit to the City of David. His mother told him to call Uncle Ronny for directions, but he didn't have to. He'd been to the Old City of Jerusalem plenty of times. He'd find the City of David in no time.

Uri got off the bus at Jaffa Gate and walked into the Old City ✳. The City of David must be somewhere nearby, he thought. The teacher said it was the core, so it must be in the middle, like the core of an apple or a pear. He started looking. He looked in the Arab market and in the Jewish Quarter; he combed the Armenian Quarter and the Christian Quarter. He even double-checked the area around the Western Wall. But search as he might, he could find no trace of the ancient core of Jerusalem.

After hours of searching, Uri finally sat down on the sidewalk. He was close to tears. I'll never find the City of David, he thought.

Just then, a boy on a skateboard rolled by. He spun to a stop next to Uri. "What's the matter, kid?" he asked. "You okay?"

"I'm fine," Uri answered, wiping his nose with his sleeve. "Just hanging out. Hey, are you from here?"

"Yes, I live in the Jewish Quarter."

"Do you happen to know where the City of David is?"

"Sure," the boy answered. "Who doesn't know that? You're in the wrong place. You have to go out of the Old City and turn left."

Uri hesitated. Leave the Old City? That didn't make sense. How could the City of David be outside the walls of the Old City? It was the core, wasn't it? But the boy seemed pretty sure of himself. So Uri got up and walked out of the Old City through Dung Gate . As he emerged, leaving the city walls behind him, he looked to the left. Below him was a small hill. Sure enough, at the edge of the hill stood a big harp and above it was a sign with the words, "City of David National Park." ✳

Finally!

Uri approached the gate and hurried through.

111

"Hold your horses, Carrot Top." Uri turned back to the gate to see a security guard motioning him to stop. "What's the rush?"

"Carrot Top" again! thought Uri angrily. Why can't people just call me by my name? "I'm looking for Professor Ronny Armoni," said Uri. "He's my uncle and he works here. I'm supposed to meet him."

"Ahh," said the guard as a smile spread across his face. "Ronny Armoni is your uncle? Why didn't you say so? Come on in." He made a sweeping gesture with his hand. "He's the boss around here, but why are you so late? All the action in the excavations happens early in the morning, before the sun comes out and the heat gets unbearable."

Uri looked at his watch. He'd wasted hours.

"Look, there's your uncle now," said the guard, pointing to a tall man approaching them.

Suleiman the Magnificent and the Old City Walls
Suleiman the Magnificent was the sultan (king) of the Ottoman Empire from 1520 to
1566. He was famous as a builder. One night, the story goes, Suleiman had a dream
that he would be eaten by lions unless he rebuilt the walls of Jerusalem. He therefore
worked very hard to build the beautiful walls that surround the Old City of Jerusalem
to this day.

Uri immediately recognized Uncle Ronny's broad-brimmed hat sitting atop a head of silver-grey hair. His tanned face was creased with small lines drawn by the sun. He seemed a little concerned.

"Uri," said Ronny. "Where have you been? I was beginning to worry."

"Something weird happened," Uri answered. "The core is supposed to be in the middle, right? Like an apple or a pear? But, somebody took the core out of the apple — I mean, out of the city. It just doesn't make sense."

"Easy, my friend," said Ronny, putting a comforting hand on Uri's shoulder. "Let's start from the beginning. You thought that the ancient core of Jerusalem was inside the Old City walls. But those walls were actually built many years after King David by an Ottoman king known as **Suleiman the Magnificent** . Suleiman built his walls about five hundred years ago. And Jerusalem from the time of the Bible goes back almost four *thousand* years!"

"Four thousand years?!" Uri imagined calendar pages flipping by at a dizzying pace. "That really is old, but then where are the original walls, the ancient ones from the time of the Bible?"

"Those walls were destroyed long ago by the Babylonians," said Ronny.

"You mean there's nothing left of David's city? I'm supposed to write a report."

"Oh, much remains of David's city, but it's all buried underneath the ground. To find the remains of the walls and the homes, you have to dig deep under the layers of earth and debris that have covered them over the years. Sometimes a city is covered by so many layers that it gets lost. That's what happened to the City of David."

"Like the lost city of Atlantis?" asked Uri excitedly.

"Well, something like that," smiled Ronny. "The search for the biblical City of David has been going on for years, with most scholars looking for it — as you did — inside the walls of the Old City. It was only about 150 years ago that **Captain Charles Warren** 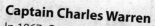, a young British officer, explored this hill and found the ancient city."

Uri was glad to hear that it was the city that had gotten lost and not him, but he was still a bit confused.

"Uncle Ronny, how can an entire city get lost? It sounds like a fairy tale."

Ronny explained. "The city of Jerusalem was the site of many battles and it was destroyed several times. Each time it was conquered, the new inhabitants razed the old buildings and built new ones on top of them. Each time this happened, the city rose higher and higher and what was left from the previous buildings sank lower and lower. Eventually the oldest levels disappeared beneath the ground altogether and the city vanished."

"So the city from the time that King David captured it from the Jebusites is still buried here somewhere in this hill."

"Yes, the hill is what we archaeologists call a *tel*. The deeper we dig into the tel, the farther back we go in history."

"Like the marshmallow base," said Uri.

"Marshmallow base?" Now Ronny looked confused.

Captain Charles Warren

In 1867, Captain Charles Warren was sent by a British group known as the Palestine Exploration Fund to learn the secrets of Jerusalem, which at the time was a small, poor city. Together with his trusted aide, Sergeant Henry Birtles, Warren explored the city's ancient ruins, which were deep underground. Warren had many adventures and difficult encounters. His most important finds were the City of David, where ancient Jerusalem started, and the ancient water system that is now named after him — Warren's Shaft.

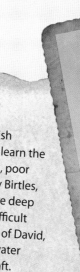

"You know that layer cake Mom makes? There's a layer of chocolate, a layer of strawberry cream, and down at the very bottom she puts this thick marshmallow base. That's the part I like best. So the marshmallow is like biblical Jerusalem — you know, the bottom of the tel. To get to it you have to dig deep into the chocolate and strawberry."

"Precisely," laughed Ronny. "I couldn't have put it better myself. Now come with me to the lookout point at the top of the hill. That's where we can get the best view of the ancient tel and its surroundings. Oh, wait. I almost forgot to give you this."

Ronny pulled out a small green notebook. On the cover were the words, "The City of David — Ancient Jerusalem."

"Your mom told me you have an assignment for school. You can use this to write down all the information you gather during your visit to the City of David."

"Thanks," said Uri gratefully. "It's perfect. I'm supposed to find out how David captured Jerusalem from the Jebusites. I'll write everything here. I already have my first piece of information."

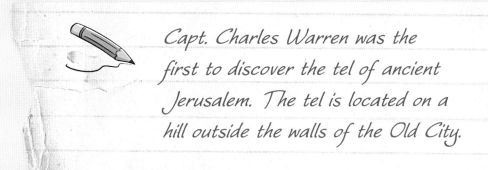

Capt. Charles Warren was the first to discover the tel of ancient Jerusalem. The tel is located on a hill outside the walls of the Old City.

Chapter **3** Uri Gathers Intelligence on the Enemy

Uri climbed the steps to **the lookout** and took in the breathtaking scenery. The afternoon breeze felt good on his face. He felt a little like a spy gathering information on the enemy. "The city is surrounded by mountains," he observed. "That makes it hard for approaching armies to get there."

"Correct," said Ronny. "And when they did reach the city, the attacking soldiers would still have to climb the hill before they could storm the walls. Look down at the Kidron Valley. The hill is very steep."

Uri hurriedly jotted in his notebook:

> Can't take Jebus from the east! Our soldiers would have to climb up the steep slope from the Kidron Valley with Jebusites firing at them from the ramparts. Too dangerous!

"Uncle Ronny," he asked, "is the hill steep on the other sides, too?"

"It used to be, though over the years some of the valleys have been filled in with earth. I'll draw you a map of what the city looked like in David's time."

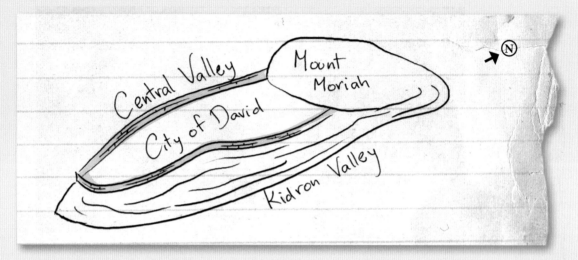

Uri inspected the map. Deep valleys encircled the hill from the south and west. He wrote in the notebook:

We can't attack from the south or west either!

Uri checked the map once more and his face lit up.

"There's still the north." He cleared his throat. "We'll take the city from the north!"

Ronny lifted his hand. "Patience, my friend, is the virtue of a wise commander. Never underestimate your enemy. The Jebusites built a mighty fortress for exactly that reason. Over there you can see the ruins of the **Citadel of Zion** ✳ 🔍 . It protected Jebus from the north."

Uri looked where he was pointing and saw a stone structure with huge boulders set one on top of another like steps.

"It looks more like a turtle shell then a citadel," Uri said.

"Only a small part of the original fortress survived. You have to use your imagination to picture what it once looked like."

"My imagination?" asked Uri. "Everyone keeps telling me I use it too much."

"Imagination can be a helpful resource if you use it properly. Just don't get carried away. Take the citadel, for instance. Try to picture its strong walls and high towers. Perched up there on top of the hill, it must have looked pretty frightening to an attacking army."

Uri was busy writing.

Can't conquer the city from the north either. The mighty Citadel of Zion protects that area.

Uri's face grew serious.

"Now what do we do? This whole hill is protected. You know, in class I had this idea — that David put his soldiers in a huge sling..."

He stopped mid-sentence.

"Never mind. Capturing Jebus seems like an impossible mission."

"Jebus certainly was a hard nut to crack. That's why none of the tribes of Israel were able to conquer it until the time of David. Let's go to the Gihon Spring. That's the city's main water source. Maybe you'll get some ideas there."

The Jebusite Citadel of Zion

They descended the steep staircase leading down to the Kidron Valley.

Halfway down the hill, Ronny stopped. He pointed to a wall built of large stones.

"This is the ancient city wall. It was built by the Canaanites in the days of Abraham, almost four thousand years ago."

Uri looked at the big, strong stones. After all those years, they still looked invincible.

"But I thought you said we were going to the spring."

"We are," Ronny answered. "The spring is outside the wall, near the bottom of the hill. Right here." He pointed it out on the map.

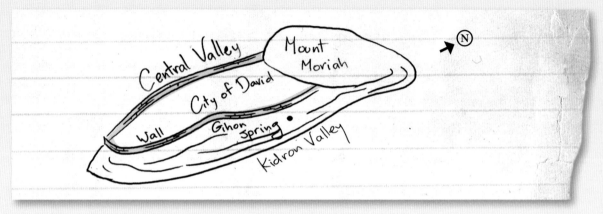

Uri scrutinized the map. An idea was forming in his mind.

"I get it now!" he exclaimed. "Since the spring was outside the walls, the Jebusites couldn't protect it. David must have captured the spring and cut the Jebusites off from their water supply!"

Ronny shook his head.

"I'm underestimating the enemy again?" asked Uri dolefully.

Ronny nodded. "The Jebusites knew they could never survive without water. The spring was surrounded with huge fortifications. Come, I'll show you."

Ronny and Uri continued down the slope until they reached the entrance to a cave. It was dark inside, and Uri could hear the sound of rushing water.

"This is the **Gihon Spring,** " Ronny said, raising his voice over the water. "People came here to fill their jugs with water. The spring is one of the main reasons the city was built here in the first place."

"Why did they call it 'Gihon?' asked Uri.

"'Gihon' means 'to burst.' The Gihon's waters usually flow at an even pace, but once in a while they burst out of the ground with great force, making a lot of noise and causing the water level to rise. Legend has it that a huge crocodile lived in the spring and swallowed its water. When the crocodile fell asleep, his mouth shut and the water rose suddenly, causing a great commotion."

Uri listened attentively. "There isn't really a crocodile in here, is there?" he asked with a forced smile.

"No, that's just the legend. But some very important things really did happen here at the spring."

"Solomon's coronation," whispered Uri, remembering what he had learned in school.

"Yes, the endless flow of the spring's water was considered a good omen for a new king. It meant he would have a long and peaceful rule."

The Crazy Spring

An old Arab legend tells of a pulsating spring that was possessed by demons. Unlike a normal spring, which flows at an even pace, this spring would burst forth suddenly, gushing with large quantities of water as if it had gone mad. The real reason for the outbursts is a law of nature that applies to rock formations that are produced in a certain way. The spring water collects in a deep cave, and when it rises to the top of the cave wall, it spills out all at once, making quite a commotion and scaring anyone who happens to be around at the time.

Uri closed his eyes. He was surrounded by thousands of people standing silently on the slopes. Near the spring was young Solomon, and standing next to him with a small flask of oil was Zadok the priest. Zadok put a little oil on Solomon's head and suddenly the quiet was shattered by the thunder of drums and trumpet blasts. A huge roar rose from the crowds, bounced off the mountains, and echoed through the valley below: "Long live the king! Long live King Solomon!"

"Earth to Uri," called Ronny. "Time to go. I'll show you how the inhabitants of Jebus protected their precious water."

Coming out of the cave, Uri saw that they were surrounded by walls built of huge stones.

"Wow, those stones must weigh a ton."

"Actually, each of them weighs three to five tons. The stones come from a huge tower the Canaanites built over the spring to protect it. They piped the spring water through a tunnel into that large pool over there."

"But Uncle Ronny, the people of Jebus would have to leave the city walls to get to the spring and the pool. Wouldn't they have been in danger from the attacking army?"

Before Ronny could answer, Uri heard a voice calling out. "Hey, professor!" Uri turned to see something that looked like a man coming towards them. He was so covered in dust and dirt that only his bright, cheerful eyes were clearly visible.

The man reached over to shake Ronny's hand. "We're about to finish clearing the earth from the guarded passage, Ronny," he said. "We're making history!"

"The guarded passage?" asked Uri. "What's that?"

"It's the answer to your question," Ronny explained. In times of war, the Jebusites used a secret tunnel under the city wall. Once outside the walls, they reached the water through a fortified passage made of two strong walls. That's the guarded passage Eli here is talking about. He and his team have just finished clearing away the debris that covered it for thousands of years."

"Secret tunnel? Guarded passage?" asked Uri. "They were pretty clever, those Canaanites."

"Clever indeed, and powerful. So powerful that when David arrived with his army, the Jebusites jeered at him from the walls. They put blind and lame soldiers on the ramparts."

"Blind and lame soldiers? They can't fight!"

"That was the point — to humiliate David in front of his soldiers. It was like they were saying, 'We are so strong that even if all our soldiers were blind and lame, David would never get through our walls.'" Ronny cupped his hands over his mouth, mimicking the Jebusite soldiers. "There's no way David can get in here," he taunted. "Even the blind and the lame can hold you back."

Uri could almost see the Jebusites mocking the young king. He heard their laughter rolling through the valley. "David can't come in here. David can't come in here. Carrot Top, Carrot Top …"

Uri clenched his fists and his face turned red. "They insulted David in front of the whole class — I mean, army! "He should have charged and let those Jebusites have it!"

Ronny held up his hand. "Patience..."

"… is the virtue of a wise commander," Uri finished.

"Precisely. Charging the walls would have brought David's soldiers under heavy fire. The Jebusites would have showered them with arrows from the ramparts. From their high position, they could have rolled down large boulders and poured boiling oil on the Israelite troops."

Uri knew Uncle Ronny was right. There would have been many casualties. He racked his brain. There had to be another way to get into the city.

"I have an idea," he said excitedly. "That secret tunnel that comes out of the city must also lead into it. Maybe David found the entrance and — "

"Hold on." Ronny put up his hand again. "You'll see the secret tunnel tomorrow. It's called Warren's Shaft. Then you can decide whether it's really the solution to your problem. And bring your Bible tomorrow. It may give us the clues we need to figure out how King David captured Jerusalem."

Uri wrote in his notebook:

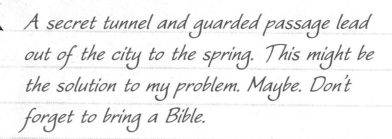

A secret tunnel and guarded passage lead out of the city to the spring. This might be the solution to my problem. Maybe. Don't forget to bring a Bible.

Uri couldn't stop thinking about the secret tunnel. That night, he dreamed he was climbing through the dark tunnel together with David's soldiers, a sword in one hand and a shield in the other.

He even saw the stunned expression on the faces of the Jebusite guards when they realized their secret had been discovered. Swords clashed. Just as Uri was about to charge forward, he heard a familiar voice.

"Uri," his mother called. "Good morning. It's time to get up."

Chapter **4** Uri Captures
the Jebusite City

Uri got ready quickly. He put his Bible in his bag, along with the notebook Uncle Ronny had given him and a sandwich his mother made for him. He couldn't wait to get to the City of David.

"Uri," his mother said at breakfast, "there's no need to gulp down your food. The ruins in the City of David have been there for thousands of years. They can wait a few more minutes."

Uri took the bus to the Old City and walked quickly to the gate of the City of David.

"You're here again, Carrot Top?" the guard called. "Good for you. I see you're a serious guy, like me." He gave Uri a high five. "What's happening today?" he asked.

"We're going into the secret tunnel," Uri answered.

"Warren's Shaft. Nice. Have a seat. Ronny will be here any minute. Coffee?"

"No, thanks," Uri answered as he sat down on a wooden bench. "I'll just read until Uncle Ronny gets here."

He took out his Bible and flipped through the pages. After the Jebusites taunted David from the city walls, the king gathered his soldiers. *David said, "Whoever smites the Jebusites first shall be commander-in-chief." And Yoav ben Zeruiah went up first and was appointed commander.* (I Chronicles 11:6).

That's interesting, thought Uri. David was offering a big reward to whoever volunteered to lead the attack against the Jebusites. It must have been a very dangerous mission. That's why Yoav volunteered. He was brave and strong.

Uri took out his notebook.

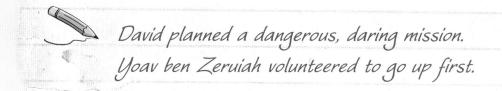

David planned a dangerous, daring mission.
Yoav ben Zeruiah volunteered to go up first.

But what exactly was the mission? And how could Yoav capture a city all on his own?

Suddenly Uri noticed a shadow on the page. He looked up.

"Are you Uri?" asked a woman wearing a broad-brimmed hat and sunglasses. She had on a T-shirt with a picture of an ibex — the emblem of the Nature and Parks Authority — and the words "Tour Guide."

"Yes," answered Uri. "Who are you?"

"My name's Meitar. Ronny said I'd find you here. I see you're reading about the capture of Jebus. Need help?"

"No. Well, maybe. I can't figure out what Yoav's mission was."

Meitar took the Bible from him. "You're looking in Chronicles. There's another description of the capture of Jebus in the Book of Samuel. Here, read this."

Uri read aloud: *"And David said on that day, 'Whoever smites the Jebusites and reaches the tsinor ...'"* (II Samuel 5:8).

"*Tsinor*?" Uri asked. "What does a pipe have to do with capturing the city?"

"*Tsinor* doesn't mean "pipe" here," said Meitar.

"Then what does it mean?" asked Uri impatiently.

Just then, Ronny arrived. "Here you are, Uri. I see you found a friend. How are you, Meitar?"

"Doing fine. Your nephew here was just trying to figure out the meaning of the biblical term *tsinor*."

"Oh, the puzzling *tsinor*. That riddle has baffled scholars for years. But I think the best place to figure it out is down in Warren's Shaft. We're going there now."

On the way, Uri scribbled in his notebook.

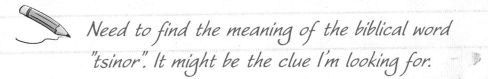

Need to find the meaning of the biblical word "tsinor". It might be the clue I'm looking for.

They soon reached a small building and walked down a steep staircase. They were going deeper and deeper beneath the ground.

"Watch your step, Uri. You don't want to reach the shaft too quickly."

Uri held on to the railing carefully, taking one step at a time. When he reached the bottom he looked up. They were in a deep, dark tunnel.

"This is the secret tunnel the Canaanites chiseled out of the rock," said Ronny. "It passes under the city walls all the way to the area with the spring and pool that we saw yesterday."

Uri looked up at the tall rock walls. Those Canaanites must have worked very hard to make this, he thought. In some places he saw holes just large enough to hold an oil lamp. He imagined a Canaanite woman with a jug on her head carefully climbing down in the flickering lamplight.

41

Ronny moved on a bit and stopped at a deep hole in the rock. Uri peered over the railing. "This is **Warren's Shaft** ✳," Ronny said. "It goes down 13 meters. It was through this shaft that Captain Charles Warren climbed when he first discovered the underground tunnels."

"Do we have to climb down the 13-meter shaft?"

"No," Ronny laughed. "No rappelling today. Just follow me. Soon we'll reach the guarded passage that Eli was talking about. That will lead us to the spring and the pool."

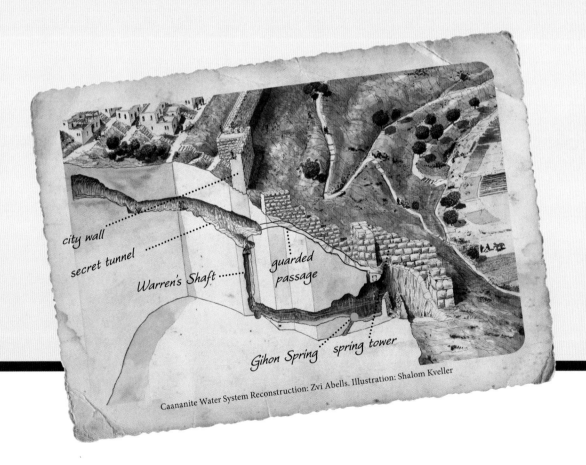

city wall

secret tunnel

Warren's Shaft

guarded passage

Gihon Spring   spring tower

Caananite Water System Reconstruction: Zvi Abells. Illustration: Shalom Kveller

But Uri remained glued to the spot. He was deep in thought.

Suddenly, his eyes lit up. "Uncle Ronny, I think I have the solution! The secret tunnel is the *tsinor*. It's a code word. The tunnel looks a little like a long pipe and it was used for getting water. David must have found out about the tunnel and decided to use it to get into the city. That's why he needed a courageous volunteer. Yoav's mission was to climb up the tunnel, taking on the Jebusite guards as he went."

Ronny smiled. "Let's assume for a moment that you're right and Yoav somehow managed to get into the city through the secret tunnel. What then? Did he take on the entire Jebusite stronghold single-handedly?"

Uri wrinkled his nose. He hadn't thought of that. "Wait! Yoav didn't have to capture the city alone. The Jebusite guards on the wall were all looking out to the valleys below, so no one knew that Yoav had already entered the city. He ran straight down to the city gate and opened it from the inside. David and his soldiers were lying low, waiting for just that moment. Yoav gave the signal and the entire Israelite army came charging through the gate, taking Jebus completely by surprise!"

Ronny looked at his nephew as if he were seeing him in a new light. "Now that is a very interesting reconstruction of events," he said.

"Has my imagination gone wild again?" asked Uri, dropping his gaze.

"Not at all. What you're saying makes sense. It fits what the Bible tells us about the capture of Jebus and the archaeological evidence of those events. In fact, similar theories have been offered by scholars. You can be proud of your imagination."

Ronny patted Uri on the back. "Your reward is that after lunch, you can cool off in Hezekiah's Tunnel ✳."

Chapter **5** Ancient Treasures and Modern Thieves

After lunch, Uri changed into rubber sandals and grabbed his flashlight from his bag. He'd heard about the water tunnel from his friends and he was eager to get inside it.

"How long is the tunnel, Uncle Ronny?" he asked.

"The tunnel begins at the Gihon Spring ✳ and follows a long, winding path to the Pool of Shiloah ✳ . It's more than half a kilometer long. It takes about half an hour to walk through."

Uri was curious. "Why did Hezekiah dig such a long underground tunnel in the first place?"

"Hezekiah was king of Judah when a ferocious empire, the Assyrians, came to power. All the surrounding kingdoms surrendered to the Assyrians, but Hezekiah chose to fight for his nation's freedom. Sennacherib, king of Assyria, was furious. He marched on Judah with an enormous army to punish Hezekiah."

Uri was listening intently. "What does that have to do with the water tunnel?"

"In order to lay siege to Jerusalem, Sennacherib would need a lot of water for his troops and horses. Hezekiah wanted to prevent him from getting that water. Here." Ronny opened the Bible. "Hezekiah 🔍 explains it himself."

King Hezekiah and the Assyrian Siege

King Hezekiah ascended to the throne of the kingdom of Judah in the late eighth century BCE when he was a young man of twenty-five. The kingdom was then paying tribute to the oppressive Assyrian Empire, and Hezekiah led his people to rebel and fight for their freedom. Being a righteous king, Hezekiah put his trust in God, but he also worked hard to protect Jerusalem from the approaching Assyrian army. Hezekiah's two great achievements were building a great wall around Jerusalem and channeling the city's water supply into the walled city. The tunnel Hezekiah built for this purpose was dug through 533 meters of solid rock and is considered to this day to be one of the great engineering feats of ancient times.

Uri read aloud:

> When Hezekiah saw that Sennacherib had come to wage war against Jerusalem, he consulted with his officials and military staff to block all the springs outside the city, and they helped him. A large group of people gathered and blocked all the springs and the stream that flowed through the land. Why should the kings of Assyria come and find plenty of water?" they said (II Chronicles 32:2–4).

"I get it," said Uri. "Hezekiah blocked the springs so that the Assyrian troops wouldn't be able to get their hands on the water."

"Precisely, but he also had to make sure the people in the city had sufficient water for their own needs. That's what the tunnel was for, to bring the water into the city so his people could draw water without fear of the enemy."

Uri closed the Bible. "Digging a half-kilometer tunnel in solid rock doesn't sound so easy."

"It certainly wasn't, and this was many years before the invention of electricity and power drills. They used simple pickaxes to cut their way through the dark tunnel. To save time, one team started from the Gihon Spring and the other from the Shiloah Pool ☀ ."

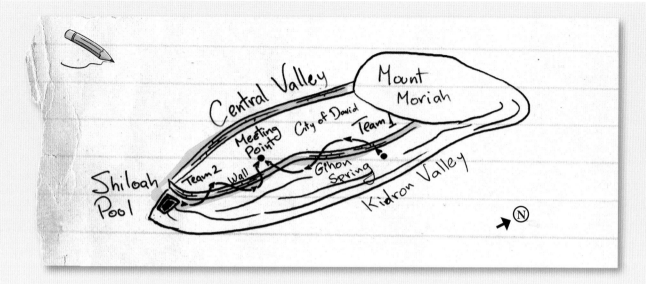

Ronny drew a picture of the tunnel in Uri's notebook. "Here," he said, pointing to a dot in the middle. "This is where they met."

Uri was incredulous. "But they were digging in solid rock! **How could the two teams of workers know where to meet?**  They could have easily missed each other."

"Ahh," Ronny sighed. "That is one problem we still haven't been able to solve. Sometimes I think the ancient engineers knew more than we do. But even for them it must have been an exciting moment when the two groups met. It says so in the inscription."

How was Hezekiah's Tunnel Built?

For years, scholars have been trying to figure out how the diggers of Hezekiah's Tunnel were able to meet in the middle. How could two groups of workers coming from opposite directions know exactly where to go without modern tools and navigating equipment? Some scholars believe that they followed a natural crack in the rock that had been there for many years. This would have ensured that they would never get lost.

"There's an inscription in the tunnel?" asked Uri.

"There used to be. It was discovered more than a hundred years ago by a boy about your age when he was exploring the tunnel. His name was Ya'akov Eliahu."

Uri nodded knowingly. Another boy sent on a school assignment. "What happened to the inscription?" he asked.

"It was stolen by antiquities thieves. The thieves were caught, but unfortunately, the inscription was never returned to the tunnel. In its place is a copy of the original. Here, take this key I've prepared for you. It will help you decipher the **ancient Hebrew** 🔍 letters in the inscription."

"But why would thieves *want* the inscription?" asked Uri.

"Relics of the past are very valuable, and many adventurers set out with the hope of finding ancient

Ancient Hebrew

Our ancestors in the First Temple period used the ancient Hebrew alphabet, in which the letters are pictures of objects that resemble the name of the letter. For example, the letter *bet* (𐤁) looks a bit like a house, which is *bayit* in Hebrew. The letter *ayin* (𐤏) looks like an eye, which is what *ayin* means in Hebrew. The letter *vav* (𐤅) looks like a hook and the word *vav* also means "hook".

treasures, gold, and silver. One famous expedition was led by a man named  **Montague Parker**. He came to the City of David from England looking for Solomon's treasures."

"Gold and silver? The treasures of King Solomon?"

Suddenly, Uri noticed someone standing behind them. It was a man wearing sunglasses, a white shirt, and a bow tie. A bow tie in this heat? Weird. Whenever Ronny stopped talking, Uri heard the man's heavy breathing. It sounded a bit like a tractor engine. Why is he following us around? thought Uri. He looks suspicious.

"Okay, Uri," said Ronny. "Are you ready to go into the tunnel?"

"But Uncle Ronny, aren't you coming with me?"

"No, I have to get back to the dig. Don't worry, though. You won't be alone. Your teacher called and asked if a classmate of yours could join you. I think that's him coming now."

Uri looked up and saw Meitar coming down the steps with a boy his age. Yoav! "*He's* coming with me?" Uri protested, trying hard to contain himself. But Ronny was already on his way. "See you later, boys. We'll meet at the end of the tunnel in half an hour. Have fun."

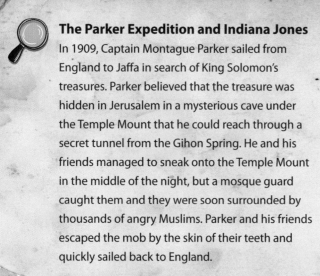

The Parker Expedition and Indiana Jones

In 1909, Captain Montague Parker sailed from England to Jaffa in search of King Solomon's treasures. Parker believed that the treasure was hidden in Jerusalem in a mysterious cave under the Temple Mount that he could reach through a secret tunnel from the Gihon Spring. He and his friends managed to sneak onto the Temple Mount in the middle of the night, but a mosque guard caught them and they were soon surrounded by thousands of angry Muslims. Parker and his friends escaped the mob by the skin of their teeth and quickly sailed back to England.

Chapter 6 Misadventure in Hezekiah's Tunnel

"Fun?" Uri muttered to himself after Ronny left. How much fun could it be to explore the tunnel with Yoav? He looked at Yoav angrily.

"Don't look at me," said Yoav defensively. "It wasn't my idea to come here, and anyway, you're the one who started the whole thing."

"I really don't feel like talking about it," said Uri. "Turn on your flashlight. We're going into the tunnel."

"Wait," said Yoav suddenly. "How deep is the water? I don't know how to swim."

"Stop whining. Didn't you see the water gauge at the entrance to the site? It doesn't go above your belt."

Uri and Yoav turned on their flashlights and waded into the cool water of the tunnel.

"Hey, this is fun," Yoav said. "The water's cold."

Uri couldn't hide his enjoyment. "Well," he said grudgingly, "maybe it does beat sitting in class. But I've got work to do. So don't get in my way."

"What are you doing?"

"I'm examining the chisel marks on the walls of the tunnel. I want to see where the two groups of workers met."

"Workers? I don't see how more than one worker at a time could fit in here. It's too narrow for more than one person."

Uri thought for a moment. "Well, the workers were coming from both sides and they met in the middle. I guess the first worker in each group chiseled forward and the others stood behind him in a row, passing back the rock pieces in baskets."

"Smart," Yoav said. "You know, it's funny, these chisel marks were made by our great-great-great-great-grandfathers. Imagine. It could have been us chiseling away if we had been born a few thousand years ago."

For a moment neither spoke. They listened to the soft lapping of the water on the walls.

"Um, Uri? Aren't you scared to be alone in here? What if something happens?"

"Stop acting like a baby," Uri said as he shone his flashlight in Yoav's face. He could see that Yoav really was afraid. He softened his tone. "Thousands of people come through here every day. There's nothing to worry about."

They continued walking through the water.

Suddenly, Uri stopped. "Quiet," he whispered to Yoav. "I think I hear something."

They stood silently. Above the rush of the water, they could hear someone breathing heavily.

Yoav laughed. "It sounds like a motorcycle."

"Quiet. I know that sound. It's that weird guy who was following me when Uncle Ronny was talking about King Solomon's treasures. He might be an antiquities thief!"

"There are thieves in this tunnel?" Yoav looked scared again. "Let's get out of here. I'm going home."

The breathing became louder. The boys quickened their pace but the sound came closer.

"Run!" Uri cried.

"I can't," Yoav said desperately. "How can I run in this water?"

The sound kept getting closer. It was almost upon them now.

Yoav began to cry.

Suddenly, Uri noticed a crack of light up ahead breaking through the darkness of the tunnel.

"Hurry! That's Warren's Shaft over there!"

"Who's Warren? Is he chasing us, too?"

"I'll explain later." They dashed forward and reached an opening in the tunnel just above their heads. "Quick, give me a boost!"

Yoav helped Uri scale the wall and get through the opening, and then he climbed up himself. The boys found themselves in an upper connecting tunnel. Uri recognized it as the shaft that Uncle Ronny had shown him from above, the one Captain Charles Warren used to explore the underground water system. The two boys sat quietly, peering down into the main tunnel below. "Now let's hope he doesn't see us," Uri whispered.

The man kept coming closer, his flashlight beaming in all directions. He reached the opening to Warren's Shaft and stopped. He was close enough to touch now. His heavy wheezing echoed loudly throughout the tunnel.

After a moment that felt like an eternity, the man moved on, working his way to the end of the tunnel. The sound of his breathing faded until they could hardly hear it.

"We're saved!" shouted Yoav, and they both breathed a sigh of relief. "Let's get out of here."

"Don't move," said Uri. "He might come back. We'd better stay here until someone comes for us."

"But I'm cold and tired. I want to go home already."

"Patience is the virtue of a wise commander," said Uri. "We wait."

After several minutes, they heard the sound of steps approaching in the water.

"Anyone here?"

Uri immediately recognized the voice of the guard. "It's me! Carrot Top!" He shouted as loudly as he could. "Remember? The kid with the red hair!"

"Carrot Top?" Yoav looked at Uri in amazement, his fear gone.

The guard looked up and shone his flashlight into the boys' faces. "There you are. You sure have been taking your time."

"We were followed by an antiquities thief," Uri explained, the words tumbling out. "He had on a bow tie and his breathing sounded like a motorcycle," the boys said together.

"An antiquities thief?" said the guard. "I don't think so. The only other person in the tunnel was an elderly tourist from England. He was trying to find you, to..."

"I knew it! I knew it!" gasped Uri. "He was after us!"

"To give you back your bag. You forgot it at the entrance to the tunnel."

Uri was glad it was too dark for anyone to see his face turn red. Once again his imagination had gotten the better of him. "Listen," he whispered to Yoav. "If you don't tell the class about this little, uh, incident, I won't tell them that you cried like a baby."

"Deal," said Yoav, and they shook on it.

The boys lowered themselves back down into the main tunnel and continued walking where they had left off, this time with the guard alongside them. At one point, Uri stopped to inspect the walls. He could see where chisel marks from one side of the tunnel met chisel marks coming from the other direction.

"This is where the two groups met!" he told Yoav.

"Boys, there's no time to explore now," said the guard. "They want to close the site for the day. Let's go."

"Patience is the virtue of a wise commander," Yoav muttered under his breath.

Soon the boys could see light shining from the end of the tunnel. The guard stopped just before the exit.

"Here's where the real antiquities thieves stole the inscription," he said, pointing to a hole in the tunnel wall. A copy of the original inscription had been placed next to the hole. Uri took out the key Uncle Ronny had given him. "Can you give us a minute to decipher the ancient Hebrew?"

"For you, Carrot Top, the world."

The boys quickly converted the ancient Hebrew letters into modern ones. Yoav read the words aloud:

> The tunnel [is complete]. And this is the story of the tunnel: As the axes pounded towards each other, and with only three cubits left to drill, the voice of a man was heard calling his friend, [for] there was a crack in the rock, on the right and on the left. And on the day of the tunnel [when the tunnel was finished] the stonecutters broke through towards each other, ax upon ax, and the water flowed from the source to the pool for [a distance of] 1200 cubits, and 100 cubits was the height over the heads of the stonecutters.

When they emerged from the tunnel, the sun was setting and a summer breeze dried their wet clothes. Meitar was waiting for them.

"Hi, guys. It took you a while to go through the tunnel. I bet it was some experience."

"You have no idea," said Yoav, with a wink at Uri, who was relaxing on an ancient pillar in the water of the **small pool** . "Is this the pool that Hezekiah built at the end of the tunnel?" he asked.

"No," replied Meitar, motioning them to follow her. "Hezekiah's Pool is still somewhere underneath the ground, but I'll show you where it once stood. The Hasmoneans, and later Herod the Great, built the magnificent **Pool of Shiloah** in its place. That was during the Second Temple period."

"Hey, we learned about that," said Uri. The boys sat down at the edge of the Shiloah Pool. "It's where the priests came on Sukkot to draw water for the Temple ceremony of Simhat Bet HaShoeva. They poured it on the altar as part of the prayers for rain, and then they celebrated all night long."

"Correct," said Meitar. "And those steps you're sitting on are part of the grand road that led from the Shiloah Pool up to the Temple. Imagine the thousands of pilgrims who came to Jerusalem for the festivals, dancing and singing as they made their way up."

Uri and Yoav stood by a huge mural depicting the site in the Second Temple period.

"I think I'm getting the hang of it," said Yoav, taking Uri's hand and dancing a little jig.

163

"Would you like to see the ancient drainage canal that passed underneath the main road?" asked Meitar. "It was used as a hideout by the Jewish rebels in the Great Revolt against Rome, and it's really interesting. The tunnel goes all the way up to the Western Wall."

"I think I've had enough tunnels for one day," Yoav answered. "Maybe we can do that some other time. But, uh, do you know where I can get something to drink?"

ancient road used by the pilgrims to go up to the Temple

drainage canal

"Up ahead is Meyuhas House . We can get some water there." As they approached, the door to opened and a woman carrying a laundry basket walked out.

"Hi, Mrs. Meyuhas," Yoav called out. "Can I have a glass of water?"

The woman laughed. "Mrs. Meyuhas hasn't lived here for quite a while. She was one of the Jewish pioneers who settled this area more than a hundred years ago. My name is Ossie. Come on in. I just made a fresh batch of lemonade."

On the wall were pictures of Yemenite Jews dressed in their traditional clothes. Ossie pointed to a picture of an elderly lady. "That's my great-grandmother. She lived here in the **Yemenite village of Kefar HaShiloah** . It was the first village established in the Land of Israel by Jews from Yemen. They built their homes across the Kidron Valley near the Arab village of Silwan."

A few minutes later, a jeep appeared, trailing a cloud of dust and screeching to a halt in front of Meyuhas House. Ronny jumped out. "Come on, boys. It's time to go home. I'll drive you to the bus stop."

Uri and Yoav thanked Ossie and climbed into the back of the jeep. The exciting things that had happened that day ran through their minds as they made their way up the bumpy road to the bus stop.

"I think you'll sleep well tonight," said Ronny as he dropped them off. "Tomorrow is your last day in the City of David, so rest up."

The First Yemenite Settlement in the Land of Israel

Although the Jews in the distant land of Yemen had strictly observed Jewish law for thousands of years, their dark skin and different customs set them apart from the rest of the Jewish community when they arrived in the Land of Israel in 1882. The fact that their fellow Jews could not believe that they were even Jewish caused the Yemenites much grief. After having lost all their possessions on the long journey, they were forced to seek shelter in burial caves on the Mount of Olives, near the Arab village of Silwan. Some time later, the local Jews realized their mistake, and with the help of the generous Moses Montefiore, they helped the Yemenites build a new neighborhood — the first Yemenite settlement in the country — Kefar HaShiloah.

7 Uri and Yoav Discover the Secrets of the City of David
(and Something About Themselves)

The next day, Yoav and Uri took the bus back to the City of David.

"Hi, Carrot Top," said the guard when they arrived at the gate. "I see you brought your friend again."

"I'm doing the assignment with Carrot Top," said Yoav. "We're in the same class. Ouch! Why'd you kick me, Uri? You called yourself that yesterday."

The guard laughed. "Don't fight, boys, don't fight. Save your strength. Go on over to the Givati parking lot. Ronny's waiting for you there. He's at the dig."

Uri and Yoav walked to the lot that was once used for parking. Now there was only a huge hole in the ground.

"Wow!" said Yoav. "That hole is the size of a football field!"

At every level of the hole stood dozens of young workers. Some were carefully brushing dust off ancient artifacts, while others were tossing buckets of earth to each other in a long chain.

"Watch out!" Yoav yelled as a bucket flying through the air almost hit Uri's head.

"Hey, kids," shouted one of the diggers. "What are you doing here? It's dangerous. We're excavating."

"We're looking for Ronny Armoni, the archaeologist," called Uri.

"He's down there," the worker answered, pointing to a winding path leading down to the bottom of the dig. Ronny was standing there surrounded by workers, examining a small, glittering object.

"Hi, Uncle Ronny," shouted Uri. "Find something interesting?"

Ronny lifted his eyes and a broad smile spread over his face. "Yes, we did. See this coin we just found? It's made of pure gold."

"Pure gold!" gasped Uri. "From the Temple?"

"No, this coin is from the Byzantine period. We've found more than two hundred of them."

"The Byzantine period?" asked Uri.

"Yes," answered Ronny. "The ancient tel of Jerusalem contains layers of life from different times and cultures. Besides the Canaanites and Israelites, the Persians, Greeks, Romans, Byzantines, and Muslims were also here. Each left their mark."

"Like a layer cake," said Uri.

"Did you say something about cake?" asked Yoav hungrily, as the three of them made their way to the visitor center.

"It's just an example, Yoav," said Uri. "One culture is built on top of another like a layer cake. The Byzantines came after the Romans, so their layer is on top, and then on top of them were the Muslims."

A Treasure of Gold in the City of David

Lots of people dream of finding gold, but not many are ever able to do it. That dream came true for Nadine Ross, a young volunteer from England who was helping with an archaeological dig in the Givati parking lot in 2008. While carefully brushing away soil in a Byzantine-period building, she found 264 coins made of pure gold. The coins had all been minted in Constantinople in the year 613 CE by the Byzantine emperor Heraclius.

"And what layer were the Japanese?" asked Yoav.

"Japanese?" laughed Ronny. "What are you talking about?"

But before Yoav had a chance to answer, they were surrounded by a large group of Japanese tourists. The tourists smiled and chatted in their native tongue as they clicked away on their cameras.

"Uncle Ronny, where are you?" yelled Uri, trying to make his way through the crowd.

He couldn't see him anywhere. Suddenly, he saw Ronny's broad-brimmed hat peeking out from above the heads of the tourists.

Uri fought his way through the throng of people. "Whew! I almost lost you," he panted. "What are these people doing here? We're pretty far from Japan."

"People come from all over the world to see the City of David," answered Ronny. "It was the center of the kingdom of David and Solomon. It's where the great prophets of the Bible like Isaiah and Jeremiah spoke their eternal words."

"Was the Bible translated into Japanese?" asked Uri.

The Bible: From Jerusalem to the United Nations
Many of the prophets in the Bible prophesied in Jerusalem. Biblical teachings spread throughout the world, and people from all over learned of the belief in one God and how human beings should behave towards one another. Isaiah, for example, called on humankind to strive for a world with no war, where all people respect each other. On a wall near the modern-day United Nations building in New York, Isaiah's words stand proudly: *"They shall beat their spears into plowshares and their swords into pruning hooks. Nation shall not lift up sword against nation, neither shall they learn war anymore"* (Isaiah 2:4).

"The Bible is revered by millions of people. It's been translated into all the different languages."

Uri wondered if the Japanese tourists knew he belonged to the people that had given them **the Bible** . Maybe that's why they kept smiling at me, he thought. It's a good thing they don't know about the trouble I got into with my Bible teacher, but that was Yoav's fault ... Wait a minute.

"Uncle Ronny, where's Yoav? I don't see him anywhere."

"There he is." Ronny pointed to a group of Japanese tourists standing in a circle around Yoav, taking his picture.

173

Yoav was busy posing for the cameras. He looked very pleased with himself.

"Come on," said Uri, pulling Yoav's arm. "We're going to the royal quarter now."

"I'm a celebrity!" said Yoav. "The crowds love me."

Uri rolled his eyes. "You really think they want *your* picture? They just chose you because you're part of the Jewish people. We gave them the Bible."

"I never gave them a Bible."

"Come on, Yoav. We're wasting time."

Yoav grudgingly left his admirers and they all walked to Area G.

Ronny said, "Here in Area G, we found remains of homes belonging to high officials of the kingdom of Judah. A thick layer of ashes covered the whole neighborhood and we had to sift through it to find the houses. We found **arrowheads** fired by the Babylonians when they destroyed the city in the year 586 BCE."

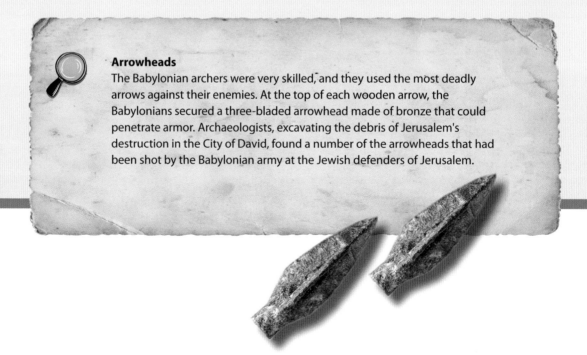

Arrowheads
The Babylonian archers were very skilled, and they used the most deadly arrows against their enemies. At the top of each wooden arrow, the Babylonians secured a three-bladed arrowhead made of bronze that could penetrate armor. Archaeologists, excavating the debris of Jerusalem's destruction in the City of David, found a number of the arrowheads that had been shot by the Babylonian army at the Jewish defenders of Jerusalem.

"How can you tell that important people lived here if everything was destroyed?" asked Uri.

"We can see from the style of the buildings, the contents, the -"

"The toilet," Yoav blurted out.

"The toilet? I told you to go when we were at the visitor center."

"No, I mean that toilet seat over there. I bet in ancient times you had to be pretty rich to have a private bathroom in your house."

Uri looked at the stone seat, which was shaped exactly like a toilet. It couldn't be, could it? "Uncle Ronny, that stone over there with the hole in the middle - is it really a toilet?"

"Yes," he answered. "It belonged to a man by the name of Ahiel whose house we excavated. Ahiel lived in a typical **Israelite house consisting of four rooms** — but his house also had an extra room for the bathroom."

The Four-Room House

In Biblical times, the Israelites built what we now call "four-room houses" or "Israelite houses." The front door opened onto a central courtyard surrounded by three rooms. In the courtyard, children played, mothers did laundry, and chickens pecked at the ground. The rooms around the courtyard were used for storage, work, and sleeping.

"How do you know his name was Ahiel?"

"We found the name inscribed in ancient Hebrew on a piece of pottery near the house. Nearby we found a large archive with many ancient Hebrew names. The archive once held important documents, but everything was written on parchment scrolls and they were destroyed when the Babylonians set fire to the city. The only things remaining from the documents were the clay seals stamped on them. Those are called *bullae*. "

"Whose names were on the bullae?"

"There are over fifty bullae. Some of them belonged to high officials who we know about from the Bible. Take this one, for instance." Ronny took a small, round disc from his pocket.

"It's a replica. You can use the key I gave you to decipher it."

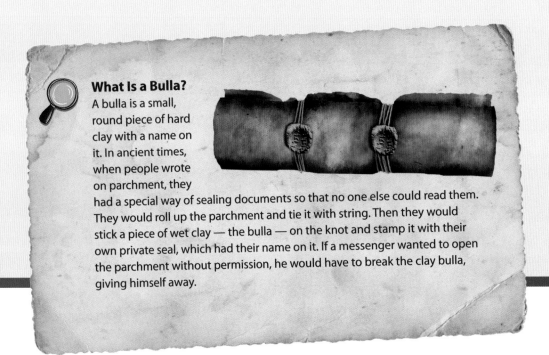

What Is a Bulla?

A bulla is a small, round piece of hard clay with a name on it. In ancient times, when people wrote on parchment, they had a special way of sealing documents so that no one else could read them. They would roll up the parchment and tie it with string. Then they would stick a piece of wet clay — the bulla — on the knot and stamp it with their own private seal, which had their name on it. If a messenger wanted to open the parchment without permission, he would have to break the clay bulla, giving himself away.

"What does it say?" asked Yoav impatiently.

"Hold on a second. I'm still deciphering ... it says, 'Gemaryahu ben Shafan.' "

Gemaryahu ben Shafan

80|

"Who was he?" asked Yoav. "I think I was sick the day we learned about him."

"Gemaryahu ben Shafan was a royal official in the kingdom of Judah," Ronny explained.

"He was a friend of the prophet **Jeremiah** who helped Jeremiah in his fight against corruption and idol worship. We also found the bullae of Jeremiah's enemies. Jehucal ben Shelemiah and Gedalyahu ben Pashhur were so angry with Jeremiah for prophesying the fall of Jerusalem to the Babylonians that they petitioned the king to have him put to death."

"Jeremiah's prophecy came true in the end," said Uri. "Jerusalem did fall to the Babylonians."

Jehucal ben Shelemiah

Gedalyahu ben Pashhur

"Yes," Ronny answered, "and Jeremiah also prophesied the return of the exiles from Babylon seventy years later. Here at the top of the excavations in Area G, you can see the exact place where Nehemiah built the Second Temple wall on top of the ruins of homes from the First Temple period. Jerusalem was built once again on its ruins."

"Like a layer cake," said Yoav.

"Like a storybook," said Uri. "Every layer in the City of David tells another chapter in the story of Jerusalem."

"Look on top of Nehemiah's wall," said Yoav. "The next chapter is about to begin and I think we're part of it."

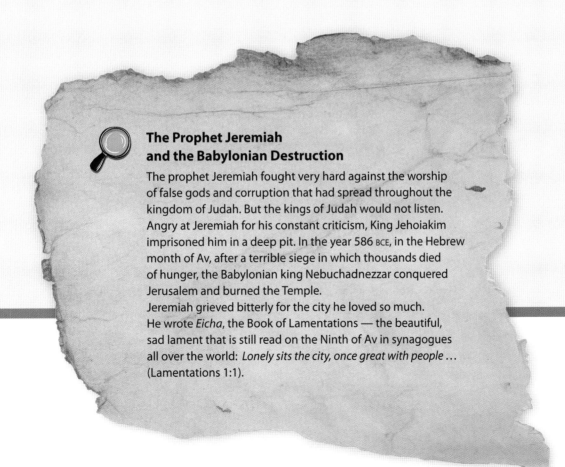

The Prophet Jeremiah and the Babylonian Destruction

The prophet Jeremiah fought very hard against the worship of false gods and corruption that had spread throughout the kingdom of Judah. But the kings of Judah would not listen. Angry at Jeremiah for his constant criticism, King Jehoiakim imprisoned him in a deep pit. In the year 586 BCE, in the Hebrew month of Av, after a terrible siege in which thousands died of hunger, the Babylonian king Nebuchadnezzar conquered Jerusalem and burned the Temple.

Jeremiah grieved bitterly for the city he loved so much. He wrote *Eicha*, the Book of Lamentations — the beautiful, sad lament that is still read on the Ninth of Av in synagogues all over the world: *Lonely sits the city, once great with people ...* (Lamentations 1:1).

"What do you mean?" asked Uri.

"That lady over there," said Yoav, pointing to the top of the slope. "She's been waving to us for the past five minutes."

Ronny and Uri looked up and sure enough, they could see someone standing by the visitor center, holding three ice cream cones and waving to them eagerly.

"That's Hadar, the site director," said Ronny. "Looks like she's got something for us."

"Ice cream always was my favorite layer," said Yoav.

"Ronny," Hadar called from above, "bring your guests to my office for a snack. I bet they'd like to cool off."

As they sat licking their cones, Ronny's beeper went off. "Oh, no," he said, reading the message. "There's been a robbery at the drainage canal! Someone stole the **golden bell** right out of the hands of the excavators!"

The Golden Bell
This little ball made of pure gold was found in the drainage canal from the Second Temple period. When the archaeologist who found it lifted it to his ear, he heard a gentle tinkling sound. He realized that he was holding a golden bell from the time of the Second Temple, possibly one that belonged to the high priest, whose robe was adorned with small golden bells.

Chapter **8** Excitement
in the Drainage Canal

"The golden bell?!" exclaimed Hadar. "Isn't that the ornament from the high priest's robe?"

"Yes, the high priest wore it while serving in the Temple. We found it today in the drainage canal near the Western Wall. Call the police, Hadar, and Uri and Yoav, go to the gate and tell the guards to keep their eyes open. We can't let those thieves get away."

"So there really are antiquities thieves," said Yoav once Ronny had left.

"Of course there are," Uri replied. "Let's go report the theft to the security guards."

As they made their way to the gate, they noticed two rough-looking men kneeling behind some bushes. One of them had a stubbly red beard, and the other was covered with tattoos.

"They look suspicious," whispered Uri.

Suddenly, one of the men pulled a small, ball-shaped object out of his pocket and placed it on the ground.

"The golden bell," Yoav said in amazement. "They're the thieves! What do we do now?"

Uri thought for a moment. "Listen," he said to Yoav, "we're going to get the bell back."

"What? Rob the robbers? That sounds dangerous."

"It won't be if you do exactly what I tell you. Your job is to distract them while I grab the bell."

"How do I do that?"

"You're an expert at distracting people. You do it all the time in class."

Yoav looked doubtful. "Come on," Uri encouraged him. "You can do it. Be brave like your namesake, Yoav ben Zeruiah."

Yoav took a deep breath. "Okay, I'll do my best." He took two steps towards the men and started yelling, "Carrot beard! Carrot beard!"

The men looked up at Yoav. "Hey, kid," shouted the burly one with the red beard. "You looking for trouble? If you're not quiet, I'll come down and teach you a lesson you never learned in school."

"How would you know, Red? You probably never went to school."

"That did it, kid. You're in for it now." As the man started moving towards Yoav, Uri quickly came in from the other side and grabbed the golden bell.

185

"Follow me!" he shouted to Yoav, as he took off at breakneck speed.

Yoav needed no encouragement. He was fast on Uri's heels.

"They're right behind us, Uri!" he shouted. "Where are we going?"

"If I tell you, they'll hear me," Uri yelled back. "Just come."

They dashed down the steep road to the Shiloah Pool ✴. "Here," Uri said softly when the men were out of earshot. "This is the drainage canal ✴ underneath the ancient road 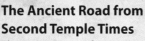 to the Temple. Meitar told us about it yesterday. She said the Jewish rebels used it as a hideout from the Romans."

The Ancient Road from Second Temple Times
The main street of Jerusalem was paved with stone and had steps leading up towards the Temple Mount. Under the street was a drainage channel. At the end of the Great Revolt against Rome, when the city was set ablaze and the Romans were killing everyone in sight, the Jewish fighters used the drainage canal as a hiding place.

"Those thieves looked scarier than the Romans," said Yoav.

The boys entered the tunnel and walked between its tall, narrow walls. Suddenly they heard footsteps from behind. "There are the kids! Hey! Give us back our bell!"

"Uri, run!" yelped Yoav. "They've found us."

"It'll be okay," Uri replied. "There's a whole group of tourists just ahead of us. We can get through faster than the thieves can." He dashed into the middle of the group.

"Excuse me, excuse me," the boys said over and over again as they squeezed through the narrow tunnel, trying not to shove anyone. The thieves were also trying to get through, but it was taking them longer to bypass so many people.

"We don't have much time," said Uri, when they had finally made it past the crowd. "They'll be here any minute. We have to reach the other end of the canal."

The boys looked around frantically. "Look!" said Uri. "There's a pulley system. The diggers must use it to haul out the big baskets of rubble from the canal. Maybe we can ..."

"Jump!" said Yoav. "They're onto us!" Uri and Yoav dove into the baskets, which started sliding quickly down the line.

"This thing is going pretty fast," shouted Yoav. "Where is it taking us?"

"To the Western Wall ✳ 🔍," Uri shouted back. "Uncle Ronny is there."

Suddenly the buckets came to a halt and strong arms lifted them up. "Hey, Ronny, look what came up in my basket," said a young, brown-haired archaeologist.

"Uri, Yoav, what are you doing here?" Ronny exclaimed. "I told you to notify the guards that the golden bell was stolen!"

"I have it," said Uri excitedly, taking the bell out of his pocket. "But the thieves are chasing us! They'll be here any minute!"

"Don't worry," said the young archaeologist. "We'll be ready for them."

Seconds later, the heads of the two thieves peeped out of the canal. Before they could figure out what was happening, they were grabbed and tied up by a team of excavators.

When the archaeologists finished tying up the thieves, they turned to Ronny. "Do you know who these boys are?" one of them asked.

"Of course I know who they are. The carrot top is King David and his friend here is Yoav ben Zeruiah."

The excavators all burst out laughing, and so did Uri and Yoav.

What Is Hiding Behind the Western Wall?

If you ask people what the holiest place in the world is for Jews, they will probably say the Western Wall — the Kotel. It's true that the Western Wall is a very important place of prayer, but it's actually the mountain behind it — Mount Moriah — that is most important in the Jewish faith.

Jewish tradition places the foundations of the world at the pinnacle of Mount Moriah, where a stone (known as the Foundation Stone) marks the beginning of creation. The Binding of Isaac took place there, too. Two temples were built on the mount. The first was built by Solomon, who requested that through this place all prayers would rise to heaven. The Second Temple was built by the exiles who returned after the First Temple's destruction. It was later remodeled exquisitely by Herod, who surrounded the mount with big walls, including the Western Wall.

Chapter **9** Dreams and Melodies in David's Palace

After the thieves were taken to the police station, Ronny, Uri, and Yoav made their way back to the visitor center.

"I think you've had enough excitement for one day," said Ronny. "Our last stop in the City of David will be a quiet one, where I hope you will be able to use your minds more than your hands and feet."

The boys followed him down a steep staircase, speaking in hushed tones. Below, they could see the natural rock of the mountain with a broken structure made of large stones ✳.

"This is David's palace," said Ronny.

"What happened to it?" Uri asked.

"The Babylonians, Uri," answered Yoav. "Nebuchadnezzar must have destroyed the palace along with the rest of the city in 586 BCE."

"Yoav is right," said Ronny. "These walls are all that remain of the foundations of the original palace. The Bible tells us that David built it with cedar wood imported from Lebanon, employing the best builders available. Nearby we found a stone capital 🔍 and a pile of well-cut bricks. The palace must have been fit for a king."

Stone Capital
The capital in this picture once stood on top of a tall column and supported the roof of King David's palace. A picture of it appears on the Israeli five-shekel coin.

"Uncle Ronny," Uri said, "Why did David choose a Jebusite city for his capital? Wouldn't it have been easier to rule from a place that had already been conquered by one of the tribes?"

"He did it to be fair," Yoav broke in. "If you want people to feel that everyone is equal, you have to choose a place where no one has the upper hand. Remember the basketball finals we played last week? The other school wanted us to play at their court, but we refused."

"Of course we did. Everyone knows the home team has the advantage."

"Right," replied Yoav. "So in the end we decided to play at Liberty Bell Park to make it fair."

Uri nodded. "That's neutral ground — not ours and not theirs."

"Exactly," said Yoav. "And that's why David chose Jebus. He wanted all twelve tribes to feel they had an equal part in his new kingdom. So he built the capital in a place that didn't belong to any of the tribes. Instead, it would belong to everyone."

"And then they would all be united," added Uri.

"Right," said Yoav.

Ronny smiled. "It's true that Jerusalem united the tribes into one nation, but even before David chose it as his capital, our ancestors had a deep connection to Jerusalem. The Binding of Isaac took place on **Mount Moriah** ✴ and Jacob foresaw the building of the Temple there."

Uri nodded. "So David didn't want a place just for his palace and kingdom. He wanted the capital to be a holy city, too. I think I heard once that the Foundation Stone on Mount Moriah is where all of creation began. It seems like everything started here."

"The City of David — The Place Where it All Began," Yoav recited, reading from a brochure lying on the floor.

Ronny's beeper went off again.

"Another robbery?" asked Yoav.

"No, I just have to run over to the office for a minute. Why don't you boys open up the Bible and read a bit more about the things that happened in David's palace?"

Uri opened his Bible and began to read.

"What?" said Yoav. "You're going to give a Bible lesson? Actually, you do look kind of like the teacher."

"Just listen," said Uri.

Uri read the story of David bringing the Ark of the Covenant up to Jerusalem - how he danced and sang with the joyous crowds while his wife Michal looked down angrily from the palace window, and how the Ark was placed in a tent in the palace court. He read about David's dream to build a great temple for God, and about how his request was refused because a temple of peace could not be built by someone who had fought so many wars.

He read about how, as David stood on the palace roof, he caught sight of the beautiful Bathsheba and about the troubles that ensued. He read about the children born in the palace: the brash Absalom, who rebelled against his father, handsome Adoniah, who tried to steal the kingdom, and wise Solomon, whom David appointed as successor to the throne and took down to the Gihon Spring to be anointed. He read about David's death and his burial in the city that he had established as the capital of Israel — the city named for him — the City of David. He read and read and Yoav listened and listened.

When he finished, Yoav said, "You know, Uri, sitting here in the City of David and reading the Bible is different from reading it in the classroom. Here, I feel like I'm inside the palace. It's as if the words were drawing pictures in my mind."

"I know what you mean," said Uri.

David, King of Israel

David, a shepherd from Bethlehem who became a king of Israel, is one of the Bible's greatest heroes. David became famous for his courage in the battle against Goliath, whom he fought without sword or armor — and beat with a single stone from his slingshot. After becoming king, David conquered the city of Jebus — Jerusalem — and turned it into the capital of all twelve tribes of Israel, uniting them as one nation. David built a royal palace in Jerusalem, and brought the Holy Ark into the city. His dream of building a temple to house the Ark would be fulfilled by his son Solomon.

The two boys were quiet. From beyond the still stones, Uri thought he could hear **David** **playing his harp**, singing the beautiful poetry of the Psalms.

Yoav finally broke the silence. "I guess that's it. It's back to school now."

"Don't remind me," said Uri, feeling disappointment wash over him.

David the Poet

Aside from being a conqueror and a leader, David was alsp a poet and a musician. People still love to read his heartfelt prayers of praise and anguish in the biblical Book of Psalms. Although he had a hard time as a ruler, he became the most famous and admired king of Israel. Today, one of the first songs that Jewish children learn is "David melech yisrael hai vekayam — David, king of Israel, lives on forever."

"Hey, Carrot Top," came a voice from above. "Why the long face?" It was the guard. He was holding a cup of black coffee.

"Oh, we're just bummed about leaving the City of David. We had a good time here."

"Of course you did. There's something about this place that touches you deep inside." He pressed his hands to his heart. "But, you know, you can take it with you."

"How? We didn't even take pictures."

"It's easy. When you want to remember your experiences in the City of David — what you learned, what you felt — all you have to do is close your eyes and think. Here, watch me." He placed his coffee cup on the railing and closed his eyes in concentration. "You think really hard and then you open your eyes and lift your hands and — ..."

Crash! The coffee cup went flying onto the rock floor, splattering the ancient stones with brownish liquid.

Uri and Yoav burst out laughing.

"What's so funny, Carrot Top? You never had coffee with King David before?"

"His name is Uri," said Yoav. "He doesn't like being called Carrot Top."

"Oh, never mind," said Uri. "I guess it's not so bad. King David had red hair, too."

It was time to leave.

"Hey," said the guard. "Let's have a high five for the City of David before you go."

The two boys jumped up to reach the guard's raised hand just as he pulled it beyond their reach. They fell tumbling down onto the grass, laughing.

"What's up with you guys? One minute you're sad, the next you're happy. Can't you make up your minds?"

The boys finally got up and said their goodbyes. They made their way to the park gate. Before passing through, they stood for a moment paused and looked at the City of David.

"Come on, Yoav ben Zeruiah," Uri said, putting his arm around Yoav's shoulder.

"I'm with you, King David," said Yoav, throwing an arm around Uri. They walked together up the hill to the bus stop.